A QUIET NIGHT, UNTIL—

" . . . The breeze stilled, the sun sank below the hill, and darkness settled in. Jed was beginning to feel drowsy, and he wished they could sleep by the campfire so the spell would not be broken. Momentarily his head nodded, but then, without warning, a piercing scream shattered the night.

"Jed's heart leaped to his throat. Terrorized, he froze in place. . . . He had never imagined such fright. For an instant, everything stood still.

"In the next second, Gretchen screamed and ripped through the embers as she raced to her father. . . ."

Bobcat!

JEANNE HOVDE

David C. Cook Publishing Co.

ELGIN, ILLINOIS—WESTON, ONTARIO
FULLERTON, CALIFORNIA

© 1978 David C. Cook Publishing Co.

Edited by Nancy Nasution
Cover illustration by Roland Dingman
Interior illustrations by Wayne Hanna
Printed in the United States of America

ISBN 0-89191-112-X
LC 78-55385

To my mother and father

CONTENTS

1

THE FENCE
BY THE
WOODS

THE UNUSUAL WARMTH of the late April afternoon made it seem more like a day in June as Jed Craig headed for the north pasture of the family farm. Staples and a pair of pliers sagged the left-hand pocket of his jeans as he walked. They rattled with each step, matching the thump of the swaying hammer against his other thigh. His gait was snappy, and he had a definite height advantage over his brother, Jared, who plodded a few steps behind. Jared was twelve, a year younger than Jed, and built much like him. He wore a T-shirt of red, while Jed's was gray.

When he reached the fence, Jed spotted the posts

and digger his father had unloaded earlier in the day as he went to the far field to plant oats. "We'll start at the corner," he told his brother. "Wherever the fence is loosening, put in new staples or pound in what's already there."

With leather-gloved hands, Jared began tugging on the wires to test the strength. "I wish there had been a little more spring instead of going right into summer," he said. "We wouldn't have to be doing this fencing."

Jed was already busy with his work. "Quit complaining. It has to be done, and it's easier when there's no foliage. The fence will be ready when the pasture is."

"I was only wishing for a little more fun this spring. That's all."

Jed pounded staples into posts that were still solid and reefed on the fence to tell which posts were rotted out. Jared trudged a few lengths to the east to begin his task.

"Get it good," Jed called. "You know what it's like when the cows get out." If there was anything he hated, it was that.

The pasture formed a wedge at the north line where they were working, and soon the boys were at the edge of the woods. Leaves that had blown in drifts along the fence last fall crunched under Jed's feet as he walked, and he glanced up into the hills where he had downed his first buck last season with great-granddad's rifle. As soon as the foliage

Mending fence was not one of Jed's favorite jobs.

came on, he wouldn't be able to see more than a few feet into the woods, but now he could see for a distance. There was no underbrush, and the tree trunks matched the brown of the leaves beneath his feet. If you had to be working, it was always nicer to work near the woods.

The sun beat warm upon his shoulders, but there was more to be done than he expected. He caught up with Jared. "Some of these posts are rotted completely off. I'll have to dig in at least six new ones." He shot a quick glance at his brother. "Unless you want that job."

Jared made an unpleasant face. "What's the second choice?"

"Go ahead and check the rest of the way."

"I'll take that."

"OK, but work. Don't fall asleep in the sun like you did with the hoeing last summer."

Jared gave him a scowl and trudged up the first incline leading to the hills above.

Jed pulled rusty staples from the first decayed post, dropped them in an empty pocket, and began digging. From time to time he heard the fence creak and felt it shake as his brother worked ahead of him, replacing and adding staples to secure the wire to the posts. Soon he was out of sight.

Where Jed dug, the soil was like hardpan, mainly because of last year's extremely dry season. Even the lake in front of their farmhouse was low, in spite of the seven springs that fed it. It was, however, not nearly as low as many of the surrounding lakes. Some had dropped as much as three feet, leaving desolate-looking banks along the shore. Nearby potholes and swamps were completely dry, and ugly, deep cracks scarred the soil below. Forest and swamp fires had followed. All through the winter the family had prayed for rain, and this spring there had been two good ones so far.

When the first rain had fallen during the night, everyone in the family had gotten up to enjoy it. They had almost forgotten what rain sounded like. Jed smiled to himself as he remembered that night a few weeks earlier. He had awakened at the sound of thunder and tiptoed from his room when the first drops began to fall.

Gretchen, his eight-year-old sister, was already in the hall, not looking the least bit sleepy. "It's raining," she whispered. "I'm going downstairs to tell mom."

Jed was wide awake too. "I'll go with you." When they passed granddad's room, they could hear him stirring. Jed went in quietly and leaned over the bed, but his grandfather was already awake.

"You heard it too," he whispered. "Help me into my wheelchair. I want to sit up and listen."

As they all entered the living room, lightning flashed, illuminating the room. Everyone was there: his parents, Gretchen, Jared, and even Sari, Jed's twin sister. They were all whispering about the wonderful sound of the rain, and Jed couldn't help but smile. "What are we all whispering for?" he asked. "There's no one left to wake up."

Gretchen swung her head around to make sure. "It seems like *somebody* should be asleep at night," she said, and everyone laughed.

"A year like the last one makes everyone appreciate the Lord's blessings more," dad said. "When they're absent, it doesn't take long to notice."

"I guess not," Jared said. "I never thought I'd be sitting up in the middle of the night listening to rain."

The lightning flashed again, and mother stood in the kitchen doorway holding a plate. "Anyone for a doughnut?" she asked. "An occasion like this is worth celebrating." No one refused, and Jed remembered how much fun it was sitting in the darkness, eating doughnuts, listening to the welcome rain, and enjoying the smiles on the faces of those around him whenever the room was lightened.

Early the next morning he had seen the season's first greenhead mallard and his mate at the edge of the lake. He knew the ducks were searching for a place to nest. It was sure to be a good season.

Jed now smiled as he dug. He always tried to remember good times while he worked. It made the work go faster and seem easier. He had already dug three holes.

He squeezed the handles together, opening the shovels, and slammed the digger into the hole. The ground would have been even harder if it hadn't been tempered by those two heavy rains. He spread the handles apart, and the shovels squeezed together, scraping over rock and dirt. Lifting the take, he piled it near the hole. It was hard work, and he mopped his arm across his forehead to dry it.

When he had finished all the holes, he set the new posts in, packed fill around them, and stapled the fence securely. He then grabbed it and shook. It was considerably more sturdy.

Jed put his gloves in his back pocket, and the hammer in the loop at his side. He swung the digger over his right shoulder and started up the hill after Jared. Here and there he saw a shiny new staple alongside the rusty ones where his brother had replaced them. Stopping atop the first rise, he called.

"Jared, are you finished?"

No answer. He must be finishing up over the next ridge.

Jed walked through the natural dip to the ridge above, where he could see all the way down to the big ravine. The cows never went beyond that, as there was little for them to eat. Still no sign of his brother.

Jed looked carefully along the fence line to make sure he hadn't fallen asleep, even though he'd been only kidding when he teased him. *The rascal!* he thought. *He finished and went home without me.* That Jared needed a prod now and then. He turned and headed for home.

Jed had put the digger in the shed and was unloading his pockets when he heard his mother calling him for supper. As he neared the house, his nostrils caught the smell of freshly baked bread, and he hurried faster. Inside, he washed quickly and went to the kitchen.

"Dad had trouble with the grain drill and went into town for parts," mother said. She was setting bowls on the table. "He said I should serve the meal so you could get ready to start the milking. Sit right down."

Jed's granddad and his sisters were already at the table. "Hurry up, Jared," Gretchen called. "I'm hungry."

Jed sat down next to his granddad and looked around the table. Meat loaf, baked potatoes, green beans, and the fresh bread. He was glad it was a good supper because he was hungry.

Sari stroked her long, dark hair impatiently. "Come on, Jared," she whined. "Supper's getting cold."

"Don't be in a hurry, girls," granddad said. "The boys have been working several hours. Give them time to clean up."

"He's had plenty of time," Jed said. "He came home a long while before I did. What's he poking

16

around with?" He could already taste the sliced meat loaf on the platter.

Mother came from the stove and stood at the head of the table, a strange look on her face. "He came home *before* you?" she asked.

"Sure. He wasn't along the fence line when I went to look, so I came home by myself."

No one said anything. Everyone stared at each other.

"He did come home, didn't he?"

Mrs. Craig put both hands on the back of the chair. "No," she said, "he didn't."

A thickness began to gather in Jed's chest, and the meat loaf didn't smell as good.

"We were outside all the time," Sari said. *"No* one came back."

But he had checked the line, and Jared wasn't there. His red shirt would have been seen easily. Jed's mind began to churn. He pictured the fence that was down and covered shortly beyond the ravine and the endless hills that stretched to the east. If Jared wasn't at the fence, and he wasn't home—

He swallowed and put his napkin back on the table. "Are you sure?" he asked.

His mother's hands were trembling. "Yes," she said, "I'm sure."

2

THE CATERWAUL

JED PUSHED HIS CHAIR BACK and stood up. "You check at the lake behind the barn, mom, on the north ridge. Yell all the way. Stay on the high spots and cover valleys on both sides wherever you can. We have to find him before dark."

"How long has he been gone?" granddad asked. "And how far could he get in that time?"

Jed thought for a moment. They left for the woods at about two-thirty, and it was nearly six o'clock now. But Jared had been there part of the time. Jed answered his grandfather. "About two hours and—and too far. He was wearing his red shirt. That's some help."

He dashed out of the house and ran toward the pasture. The sun was beginning to lower in the west. *You'd think Jared would know enough to follow the sun,* he thought. But if he knew, he'd be home.

Jed hurried all the way to the ridge that looked over the big ravine and started down the hill. Surely his brother wouldn't cross the ravine. The cows never did, so they never fenced beyond it. Everybody knew that.

The ravine ran north and south and was wide at the bottom. He raced across and started up the other side. At first the fence was still in decent shape, but halfway up, it changed. He saw a drying pole propped against it for steadiness. His heart skipped a beat. It was Jared's work.

He *had* crossed the ravine. Now he could be anywhere.

Jed ran ahead, straining his eyes for any sign of tracks in the thick, brown gray mat that made up the floor of the forest. He saw nothing. Near the top of the ridge, the fence was completely down, but a foxhole in the side of the bank caught his eye. The yellow sand that had been displaced in digging the hole contrasted with the all-brown background. He ran closer to look. Fresh tracks and finger markings were in the sand. Jared had been there.

Beyond that, the fence was buried under decaying leaves for several rods. Further on, he picked up signs of it again, here and there attached to a tree or a post that had managed to survive years of weather. But there was no sign of his brother.

How could he possibly know which way to go or where to look? Why would Jared continue at all? He stopped and prayed for guidance, then cupped his hands and yelled. Shutting his eyes to improve his concentration, he strained for an answer. None came.

He called in all directions. When he called toward the south, he thought that at least his mother would answer, and then he would be sure that the distance between them was covered. But there was no response there either. Perhaps no one could hear as far as he hoped.

Again he called to the east and thought he heard something in the distance. He yelled another time and waited. No. There was nothing. His imagination was playing tricks; he wanted an answer so badly.

Jed forgot the calling and hurried toward Flat Tail Lake. Jared had been there with him once. He didn't remember how long ago, but if he came upon it, he might recognize it. As he passed the oaks with the big red X's that marked the end of their land, he hoped Jared might have seen them and left some sign, but there was none.

At Flat Tail Lake he looked all around the west side. Still no sign. He had to make a decision—to go north or south. He decided on north. That would be the worst way for a lost person to go. You could wander for days and never find a road. There were endless acres. South, you would eventually come to something—if you went far enough in a straight line.

The ground he traveled was a continuous series of valleys and ridges, and tough as he was, his legs were tiring. He didn't usually run in the woods the way he was doing now. At the top of every ridge he stopped and called.

When Jed had gone as far north as he had intended, he stopped. To go beyond into an area he did not know would be foolish. Darkness would overtake him, and he would be lost too. Again he prayed and yelled, then held his breath and listened.

He thought there was a faint answer coming from somewhere. Cupping his hands, he yelled again, "Over here! Over here!"

There *was* an answer. Jed didn't move a step. "Over here!" he yelled again. He wanted to run in the direction he thought the voice came from, but the answer was getting stronger, and instinct told him to stay in the high spot where he could be seen.

Finally he heard the words clearly. "Where are you?"

"Keep coming!" Jed yelled. "Listen, and keep coming." He continued to call. A red dot appeared around the side of a far hill, and Jed ran toward his brother.

Jared's face was tear-stained. He was covered

with bites, and he looked ready to drop—but he was found.

"Follow me," Jed said. "We have to get out before dark." He struck a course by the fast-sinking sun, and behind him, Jared kept up. As they reached the edge of the woods and entered the pasture, Jed yelled, and an answer came from the porch.

"John!" he heard his mother call. "He's found." She and his sisters ran across the garden plot and apple orchard to the pasture fence. Jed climbed through and held the wires apart for his brother. Jared's dark, soulful eyes told that the sight of home was a great comfort.

Gretchen's face was as stained as Jared's. "I was crying," she said as she grabbed him.

"So was I," Jared said. He hugged her too.

No one mentioned that they could tell by the smears on his cheeks. Tears were in Sari's eyes too.

Mother squeezed Jared hard. "I was so worried about you, Jared. Thank the Lord, Jed found you."

They hurried to the porch where granddad waited in his chair. Dad was there too. He had turned and come from the big hill when he heard the call.

"Why did you go so far?" Jed asked. "There wasn't even a fence there, at least not one you could see."

"There was for a while," Jared said.

"Not beyond the foxhole where you were playing."

22

"I wasn't playing. I was looking for a fox."

"But you should never go past the big ravine," Jed scolded. "The cows don't. That's why there isn't any fence."

Jared looked up. "How was I supposed to know that? Which one is the big ravine? It's one hill and ravine after the other."

Mr. Craig sat on the steps and pulled Jared down beside him. "I think I see the problem," he said. "Maybe I never took the time to tell you about that." He turned to Jed. "Did you tell him not to cross the ravine?"

"No. I just thought everybody knew that. I was digging, and I forgot all about him," he admitted.

Jared wiped his eyes. "I almost went back when the fence got so weak, but I didn't think I should quit working. Then I saw another foxhole, and after that I couldn't find anything."

"What did you do then?" his father asked.

"Kept going. I thought the fence was bound to show up somewhere if I went straight."

"Didn't you know you were lost?" Jed asked.

"After a while, when I couldn't find anything. It all looked alike. Then I got scared. I lined up with a broken tree and walked away from it to see if I could recognize anything. I came back and tried another way, but the fourth time out I lost the tree."

"Why didn't you follow the sun?" Jed asked. "It always goes down in the west."

His father stopped him from saying more. "Because we haven't told him how to handle himself in the woods. He must have a chance to learn some things this year." He turned back to Jared. "What then?"

"Just walked, I guess, and cried and prayed. I saw three lakes but didn't recognize any of them. After a while I came to an old fence. I took it one way, but it faded out. I took it the other, but that quit too. It did bring me to an old trail, and I was following that when . . ."

He looked uncertainly from one to the other.

"When what?" his father asked.

"You won't believe me. You'll laugh."

"No one is going to laugh at you, son. What happened then?"

Jared put his hands together in his lap. "I was in the valley. I had come down this steep hill, and I was so tired I thought my legs would fall off. But all of a sudden I heard a terrible scream, and I shot straight up the hill. I know I went faster than a car. It was terrible, dad. Honest."

Jed started to smile, but he held it back.

Granddad leaned forward in his chair. "What did it sound like?"

"It was a lady's scream, bloodcurdling. It made the hair on my arms stand straight up."

Granddad eased back in his chair like an authority. "A caterwaul," he declared. "Appears there's a bobcat in the woods."

Gretchen ran to his side. "Oh, granddad, would it eat Jared?"

Granddad put his arm around her. "It isn't likely, child. But a bobcat is something to look out for."

She backed up and looked at him. "I thought you said a *caterwaul*."

"A caterwaul," granddad repeated, "is a noise a bobcat makes. It's quite a sound. My hair has stood on end every time I've heard it."

"Where would a bobcat come from?" Jed asked. He'd never heard of any around there.

"Hard to know," granddad said. "Might be last fall's fires forced him out of the back country. We'll have to keep a sharp lookout."

3

GRANDDAD
REMEMBERS

THAT NIGHT JED LOOKED over at Jared in the bed next to his. He had fallen asleep the minute his head hit the pillow. Jed honestly felt sorry for him. His legs must have put on many miles. But at least now he could rest. If he hadn't been found, there would be no rest for either of them, especially Jared, with all those mosquitoes and that bobcat in the woods.

Jed wondered if it was really that scary. Granddad seemed convinced, and he should know, but maybe he was *real* young when he heard it.

On the school bus Monday morning, he waited for Emery, his best friend, to board. Every time

Emery got on the bus it made him feel good. Last year he was five inches taller than Jed, but now he had quit growing, and Jed was catching up. He thought he was putting on weight too.

"Boy," he said as Emery came down the aisle and plopped in the seat beside him, "did we have some excitement over the weekend."

"Yeah? Doing what?"

"Jared got lost in the woods, and—"

His lanky friend didn't let him finish. "You call that excitement? I thought maybe you went into town and met a new girl or something."

Same old Emery, playing the big shot.

"OK, it's not the kind of excitement you like," Jed said, "but it *was* exciting. While he was out there, he heard this terrible scream."

Emery's eyes widened. "Don't keep me in suspense! Somebody was being murdered right there in front of him!" He made a disgusted face. "Come on, now."

That bugged Jed. "Jared wasn't making it up. He heard it. My granddad said it was a caterwaul."

"There aren't any caterwauls around here."

Jed looked him straight in the eye. "The caterwaul is the sound. The animal that makes it is a bobcat."

Emery looked embarrassed, but only for a moment. "Bobcats in this country? Hey, everybody!" he howled.

Jed let it go at that, but the bobcat subject became even more interesting as he thought about it, and that evening after chores he intended to ask his grandfather more. As he left the barn, he saw granddad, Gretchen, and Sari working near the clothesline. From his wheelchair, granddad was spading around the post. It was awkward, but he liked to do all he could. Gretchen held a packet of morning glory seeds in her hand.

"You always raise morning glories, don't you, granddad?" Jed asked as he neared. He had seen them in granddad's garden as long as he could remember.

Granddad stopped spading and smiled. "Always. They remind me of things."

"Like what?" Jed asked.

"Like the spring your grandmother and I were married. We lived in quite a shabby place at first. Your grandma was young, but she was always fixing things up, and she planted morning glories outside the kitchen window. One morning when we sat down for breakfast, lo and behold, one of the flowers had grown right through the wall and was blossoming at our table."

"Right through the wall?" Gretchen asked.

"Yes, ma'am. Came right through that rickety wall. Reminded me of my young wife. She was a morning person, always up and eager."

"And after that you always raised morning glories," Jed concluded.

Granddad nodded. "Even after we could afford a

better place." A wistful look crossed his face. "And now that your grandmother is gone, it means even more. Though I don't see her, I know she's blossoming on the other side of God's wall, just like that first morning glory."

Gretchen had been standing quietly by the chair. "You know what? I bet grandma's raising morning glories too."

Granddad began spading again. "Wouldn't surprise me at all. Probably come up better than mine, too, especially if you girls don't shake up that sod and work the ground a little better."

Gretchen opened the packet of seeds, and Sari planted them as granddad instructed. Then she smoothed the soil over them and packed it lightly.

When they had finished, Jed turned the wheelchair around. "I'm taking granddad for a walk. You girls put the tools away." Pushing the chair, he walked north a short way along the blacktop road, then turned and came back toward the farm. The view was beautiful, and he stopped where they could see the reflection of the buildings in the water and look into the hills above.

"What do you know about bobcats, granddad?" Jed asked.

His grandfather rubbed his chin and knit his eyebrows like he always did when he was trying to remember. "Not a whole lot, Jed. I do remember years ago, some young fellows lived next door and had a couple of snappy hounds. One night they were out coon hunting when the dogs hit trail. The boys stayed with them, and they were pretty close to having something treed when a shriek lit through the woods that scared them stiff. The story goes that the dogs turned tail, lit out of the woods with the boys after then, and none of them would go back again. Scared the hair right off the boys' heads, or so folks said."

Jed looked up into the woods. He didn't feel completely brave.

"Another time," granddad continued, "neighbors around were losing lambs and thought it was the work of wolves. But when an old fellow down the road heard his dogs giving tongue, he saw a bobcat leap to a tree and shot it. It was a big one, nearly five feet long. Weighed fifty pounds."

"Five feet long! I didn't think they were that big."

"Most aren't. Three feet or less is probably more the average, and maybe thirty pounds."

"What color are they?" Jed asked.

"A tawny brown with black spots; they have a bounding gait and can leap into the lower branches of trees. Most any cat has a lot of spring in his legs. You know that."

He wanted to ask if a bobcat would attack a person, but he hated to. He wasn't sure if he was scared, and less sure if he wanted to find out. Instead, he started pushing granddad back toward the house.

In the yard, lying half in and half out of her doghouse, was Flog, the old brown-black coon hound Uncle George had given Jed last fall. "Think Flog could handle a bobcat?" Jed asked.

"Handle one?" granddad said. "Old men and old dogs are good for some things, Jed, but not everything." He brushed his hair back from his forehead the way dad always did. "Could probably tree one, if she could keep up long enough, but if it came to a tussle—" He shook his white head slowly. "No, I don't think she'd have much of a chance."

4

A LAND
TO PROTECT

JARED'S DESCRIPTION OF THE caterwaul, plus the
picture granddad painted, had aroused Jed's
curiosity. Over and over he tried to imagine how a
bobcat would sound; but as hard as he tried, he
could not make up anything as hair-raising as
they had described.

He'd never been frightened deer hunting. Of
course, deer didn't scream. They ran away, but he
wasn't sure a bobcat would do that. And he wasn't
sure he would attack, either.

Granddad did say his accounts were stories, and
he'd admitted he didn't know a whole lot about
them. Emery had laughed it off, and maybe he was

more on the right track than the others. It was just possible that Jared's imagination was working overtime, though Jed wasn't ready to say so yet.

Dad had promised him the next Saturday afternoon off, so Emery came over. The boys decided to take a walk in the woods.

"Let's go where Jared was lost," Emery said. "Maybe we'll see that bobcat he talked about."

Jed agreed. It would be a chance to see for himself.

They headed north through the pasture, alongside the cranberry swamp, and into the first level of hills that stretched toward the northeast. As they neared the big ravine, a red fox darted in front of them and disappeared around the sidehill.

Emery halted and whistled through his teeth. "Wow! I'd sure like to get my hands on that hide."

"Why?"

"It's worth plenty, that's why."

"You need the money?"

"Sure, I need it. There are all kinds of things I want."

"But do you *need* it?" Jed couldn't see killing an animal for a whim. "Seems his life must be as valuable to him as yours is to you."

Emery shook his head. "Jed, you must be the preacher of the century!" He looked around. "Where's that Flat Head Lake, anyway?"

"Flat *Tail*," Jed emphasized. "Past the end of our land." He started hiking again. "We'll have to move if we're going back there."

Emery plopped down on the leaves. "Forget it," he said.

"I thought you wanted to see where Jared was lost."

"I don't care if I see it. I doubt that he heard a bobcat, anyway. I just wanted to get out of sight for a while."

Jed knew Jared had heard a bobcat, or something they thought was one, but why argue? This was supposed to be a pleasant afternoon. Wanting to be out of sight he could understand. He liked being alone sometimes too. Leaning against a large oak, he slithered down the trunk and used it for a backrest. Hearing the snap of a twig on the far side, he turned to look. Whatever it was had disappeared. He was still peering curiously through the brush when a whiff of smoke crossed his nostrils.

Jed whirled. Beside him, Emery held a cigarette in his mouth and a lighted match in his hand.

Without thinking, Jed grabbed his wrist. "You can't do that!" he shouted. "The woods are as dry as kindling. In minutes the whole place could be in flames and take our farm with it." He yanked Emery's hand toward him and blew out the match. "Didn't you see what the fires did last fall?"

Emery casually brushed him off. "What are you so excited about?" he drawled. "That was last fall." The cigarette had dropped from his mouth. He picked it up and replaced it. "It's rained since then." And he struck another match.

Either Emery didn't understand the seriousness of the situation, or didn't want to, but Jed thought of the hundreds of black and ugly acres he had seen. One swamp near home had burned from August to November. "Put it out!" he demanded.

Emery started to laugh. He squinted at Jed, studied the match for a second, and deliberately held it to a leaf on the covered ground.

Jed threw himself over Emery's arm and rolled to the ground on top of the lighted match.

Caught off guard, Emery tumbled behind him, but Jed rolled and was on top of him instantly. " I said *not here*. If you want to smoke, that's one thing, but you're not going to set our woods on fire." He rose to his knees and let go of Emery.

"I wasn't going to set your woods on fire. Can't you take a joke?" He sat up and brushed himself off. "I don't smoke. I just got hold of this package and thought we could have some fun trying it out. I didn't know you'd be such an old stick-in-the-mud."

"And I didn't know you'd be so reckless," Jed said. "Let's go home."

"Wrecked a perfectly good afternoon," Emery muttered as he trudged out of the woods behind him. "I'm going over to Gerald's. Maybe he has a little more life in him."

Jed didn't care. He was glad when he was back home and Emery had left. He decided not to tell his folks about the incident. Emery had said he didn't really smoke anyway, and Jed believed it.

That night it rained again, a real downpour, and on Sunday morning, Jed could almost see the grass turn green. Oats that had been planted only days earlier had sprung from the ground. Buds had appeared on the trees, and yellow daffodils had bloomed. Even the lake water level had risen.

The ground felt alive and springy beneath Jed's feet as he and his father walked to the fields and looked over the cropland after church. Most of it was level, and the new green of the stretching oats was an especially welcome sight.

"Our prayers are being answered," dad said. "Warm sun and steady rain mean a good crop." He put his hands in his pockets and looked around. "But," he added, "I wish I had more open ground for corn."

"What about that north piece?" Jed asked. He pointed to the one hilly field that was in crops, way to the north. "It raises good hay; it should raise good corn."

"It's a temptation," dad admitted. "But I really don't dare."

"Why?" Jed asked. He couldn't see anything wrong with it.

"Erosion," dad said. "If that piece was opened, one good rain would start washing it away; and when topsoil's gone, it's gone forever. This way the sod holds and preserves it." He put his hand on

Jed's shoulder. "For you, and your son."

Jed looked up at his father. "Is that really the reason?"

"It's why I try to plow as little as possible on the hilly sections. One spring I had a lot of ground plowed. But the weather turned hot and dry before the crops started coming up. Then the winds came, and the soil just took off. Day after day your mother and I watched it go. We were both sick. Finally it rained and the growing began, but I'd lost a lot of top soil."

"It's all right, dad," Jed said.

Dad shook his head. "It's never all right when you misuse something. Sometimes you have to put your own ambitions aside. It isn't always easy."

Losing a little soil to the wind didn't seem nearly as bad to Jed as what could have happened yesterday in the woods.

5

DEMOTED

A WEEK WENT BY, and Jed and his father were so busy he almost forgot about the bobcat and his differences with Emery. May was not his favorite month, anyway. There was too much to be done. Teachers, hoping to cover class material to the end of the textbooks, were pushing harder, and the summer schedule of longer work hours on the farm was already in full swing. Jed could handle one or the other, but both were almost more than he could tolerate. He also needed extra hours to finish his gun rack for woodworking class. Where would they come from?

By mid-May he felt ready to collapse, and probably would have if it hadn't been for his mother's good cooking that gave him the energy to keep going. When he and his father came in late from the field and he still had homework to face, the fresh rhubarb pie perked up his spirits and seemed to help him get his work done.

All the fence had been mended, and when he and dad walked the pasture to check it out, Jed noted that much of the white clover had died. He wondered if it would come back with plenty of rain, but dad said he didn't think so. It would have to be planted again when the time came for that field to be reopened.

On Saturday the strawberry and raspberry patches had to be cleaned, the garden planted, and the last cornfield disced. Jared would be helping mother and the girls in the garden. Jed prepared to do the discing while his father finished the plowing. He was leaving for the field on the tractor when dad signaled him to stop.

"I just remembered," he said, "we decided to give Jared a chance to do some learning this year. We'll start with the discing. This is a good flat field, easy to learn on. You won't mind helping mother this morning, will you?"

Jed stepped off the tractor. "No, I guess not," he said. But he felt a twinge of resentment as Jared ran toward it. It seemed he was being demoted.

Jared's face was filled with anticipation. He jumped on the tractor and listened as his father went through the instructions. "Let the clutch out slowly," he finished. "Drive in second gear until you get the feel. Anything I've forgotten, Jed?"

Jed started to say no, but changed his mind. "If you feel it pulling hard, raise the disc earlier rather than later," he told Jared. "Once you're stuck, it's too late."

Jared gripped the wheel and cautiously released the clutch. The tractor jerked ahead, and the motor died.

A grin crossed Jed's face, while Jared didn't look like he was having much fun.

"It's all right," dad said. "Put the clutch in, take it out of gear, and start it again."

That time Jared got it moving with a minimum of jerking, and dad hopped on the second tractor. As Jared came to the end of the drive, a car approached from behind the big trees to the south. Jared slammed on the brakes. The big tires skidded, and dad nearly ran into him.

Mother rushed from the house. "What on earth is going on?" she called to Jed. "What's Jared doing? Why aren't you on the tractor?"

"Jared's getting his chance" was all Jed said.

The motor had died again, and dad jumped off and once more helped him start it. Walking toward the tractor, Jed saw the perspiration on Jared's face and arms, and he didn't feel so resentful. He leaned over the tire and spoke to his brother. "When you let the clutch out, nothing happens at first. Just when you think it's out, you reach the

"Drive in second gear until you get the feel."

friction point and it takes hold. That's when you jerk."

Jared nodded. It went better that time, and his father followed him down the road.

Jed turned to his mother. "Remember dad said Jared should have a chance to learn? Well, today's the day. I'm supposed to help you in the garden."

Mother looked down the road after them. "I remember," she said. "It seemed like a good idea when we talked about it, but right now, I'm not so sure."

"It'll be all right," Jed said. "I did the same thing on my first try."

"Then let's concentrate on the garden," she said.

Jed did the rototilling while his mother raked to make a smooth seedbed. Then he measured and set the guides for the rows. Sari and mother did the planting, and Gretchen helped with the big seeds, the peas and beans. Then Jed covered them.

He could hear the big tractor snorting, and from time to time, the small one buzzing along as it circled the open field.

Jed looked at his mother. She was on her knees, crawling along the row because getting up and down was too hard, and putting the tiny seeds into the ground. He tried to tell himself that gardening was not a humiliating job. Mom did it every year, and granddad, with all of his wisdom, wasn't above it. He put the hoe back in the ground and made another row.

At noon when the "men" came for lunch, Jared's face and back were covered with dust, and beneath the dirt he was sunburned. But his look of pride could not go unnoticed.

Gretchen was already waiting at the table. "Did Jared run into the fence like Jed did when he first tried?"

Jared glanced at the others. "Almost," he admitted.

"I think that's enough for the first lesson," dad said. "Jed can work the field this afternoon."

That day Jed tried harder than ever. He worked the dead furrow many times, sometimes in a criss-cross swing down the field and back again to make a figure-eight design. He set the disc just right to turn in the soil and level the furrow.

"A good job," dad said as he inspected before they took the machinery home. He squinted as he peered down the field. "Can't even see where the dead furrow was."

"Thanks," Jed said. He thought he had done well too.

That evening when they were finishing chores, Emery and his dad, Harold Daager, drove into the yard. A four-wheel drive, like the one they owned, was one of Jed's dreams for the future.

Mr. Daager slammed the door on his side, rounded the front end of the truck, and stalked into

43

the barn. In one glance, as always, he surveyed everything in sight. "Evening, John." He nodded toward the manger. "Hay looks a little stemmy. Ought to try cutting it early."

Jed supported himself by leaning on the fork. No wonder Emery was Emery.

"This is the last I bought," dad said. "Not what I wanted, but what I could get. I'll be cutting the first crop when there's a good forecast."

Mr. Daager cut him off. "I didn't come to talk hay. One of my cows freshened in the pasture last night. We can't find the calf. Don't know if it's wolves or a pack of dogs, but the calf is gone. Was your hound home last night?"

"Old Flog?" dad asked. "She's always home, tied right there at the doghouse." He pointed to where she lay in the shade. "But it could be a bobcat. Jared heard a shriek in the woods he described as a caterwaul."

"A cat in the woods and you don't bother to tell your neighbors?" Mr. Daager took a step toward Jed's father. "And I lose a prize calf!"

Jed ran toward them. "I told Emery right after it happened."

Mr. Daager spun toward them. "If Emery knew, he would have told me."

"He didn't believe me," Jed said. "He laughed."

Everyone looked at Emery. He shifted his weight self-consciously and scraped his shoes on the concrete. "I wouldn't make plans around anything Jared heard," he mumbled. "He's scared of his own shadow."

Mr. Daager whirled around and motioned toward the door. "Get moving," he said to Emery. "We're going home."

After they left, Jed had a question. "Why does Mr. Daager talk to you that way, dad—like he knows everything?"

Dad smiled. "Don't let it get to you, Jed. He doesn't mean anything by it. Harold's a good neighbor."

A NEW
JOB

JED WAS NOW MORE CONCERNED about the bobcat. His family certainly couldn't afford to lose any
calves. Besides, it made the woods seem unsafe.
His family liked to spend time there for fun and
relaxation as well as picking berries.

Jed wondered if it was even safe for the cows in
the pasture. "Do you think we dare let the cows out
with that thing on the loose?" he asked his father.

"I don't think a cat would attack a full-grown
cow," dad said. "When we have one ready to
freshen, we'll keep her inside."

"What about berry picking? It won't be safe for
mom and the girls."

A New Job

"Bobcats are active mostly at night," dad said.

"But Jared heard it in the daytime."

"Yes, but he was way back in."

"I suppose I could camp near the woods and watch for him," Jed suggested.

"No," his dad answered. "We've got work to do. He probably covers a lot of ground anyway. Might be weeks or months before we hear of him again."

Jed didn't argue. He wasn't convinced they'd heard the last of the bobcat, but he wasn't sure he wanted to meet him in the dark, either, especially not alone.

School closed the next week, which was a great relief. On Monday the hay had to be cut as soon as cattle feed was ground. Jed was shoveling corn into the grinder driven by the tractor motor when the belt flew off and the grinder plugged. He ran to slow the motor, and dad hurried to examine the machine.

His father's face showed discouragement as he looked up at Jed. "A bearing went out. Another big job, and another slow start for the day. There's all that hay out there to be cut, and a good forecast."

"I'll cut," Jed said, "while you fix the grinder." He had never operated the mower-conditioner, but he had driven the big diesel a couple of times, and he didn't think cutting would be that much of a problem.

Dad looked at him doubtfully. "Think you can handle it?"

"Everyone has to learn," he sang.

Dad grinned. "OK, I'll show you how."

Jed unhooked the grinder, hopped the two steps into the cab of the diesel, and plunked down in the seat. There were three steps to remember before starting: put the clutch in, adjust the fuel lever, and turn the key. He pushed the starter, and the big engine snorted to life. Jed put it in gear and steamed ahead. At the cutting machine he shifted into reverse, backed to the hookup, and connected the power take-off and hydraulic hoses.

Dad hopped in with him. "I'll cut one round and the back swath to open the field. Watch how it's done."

It looked easy. All he had to do was turn the machine on and cut away. On the back swath, dad maneuvered around the utility poles and other close quarters with ease. The hay lay flat and neat behind him.

When he finished, he stopped and jumped out. "Any questions?"

"I don't think so." He wouldn't have to worry about any close quarters.

"OK," dad said, "go to it." And he left.

Jed leaned back and put the power take-off in gear. With the powerful machine beneath him, he felt like a king. He was glad he had washed the cab windows yesterday because he could see all over.

Letting the clutch out, he pulled ahead and topped the hay. He had forgotten to lower the machine! He shifted and backed, but the mower swung to the side, and he couldn't back far enough. So he lowered the hydraulic and pulled ahead, but for several yards, long stems stood up behind him.

He was surveying the splotchy mess over his right shoulder when he realized he was veering to the side and cutting only half a swath. He jerked back on course, but before he came to the corner, the sickle plugged. Jed backed again to clean it and left a heap of hay that would never wilt.

When he started forward, the same blotching occurred. The collar of his shirt began to tighten, and it itched around the band of his cap. Cutting wasn't nearly as easy as when dad did it. It was a long two hours till lunch, and he was glad when Jared finally came to call him.

Dad was at the table when he walked into the kitchen. "How did it go, Jed?"

Jared didn't give him time to answer. "You should *see* the field. It looks like the haircut Gretchen gave old Prince before he died."

Jed almost sank into the floor. He could still picture the old, hairy dog looking like a moth-eaten mess, with digs and nicks in some places, bristled hair in others, and loose hair bunched all over. Everyone else was laughing.

"It's not easy the first time," dad said. "A new job never is, but you'll get the hang of it."

Jed wasn't so sure. He wished dad would take the afternoon shift, but the grinder wasn't fixed yet. He passed the bread, but Gretchen didn't take it from him. Instead, she leaned back in the chair with arms folded and a hurt look. Jed studied her small, pouting face. "What's wrong with you?" he asked.

"I want a new job," she insisted. "Everybody is getting a new job but me."

"I know," Sari said.

"The problem is," mother explained, "that all the old jobs have to be done too."

Gretchen still pouted. "I know that, but I want a job all by myself."

Mother thought for a moment. "How about the egg job—all by yourself?"

"Sure," Sari said. "She's braver than I am about chasing the hens off the nest, anyway."

"You'd have to get all the eggs," mother warned. "If one hen starts laying outside, the eggs must be found."

Gretchen unfolded her arms. "I'll take it," she announced. "The only one I don't like is that old rooster. He keeps that big eye zeroed on me all the time. But I'm not scared of him—I don't think."

They all laughed again.

"Tomorrow," granddad said, "we'll have a report on your new job."

The afternoon went not much better for Jed than the morning. By suppertime he was exhausted, but in spite of that, he had difficulty going to sleep at bedtime. When he did, half the night was spent engaging the power take-off, slamming the clutch, and raising or lowering the mower. Once he jolted himself awake, his arms and legs all going in different directions. He was still tired when morning came.

"Might as well finish the cutting," dad said after breakfast.

Just what Jed was afraid of! It almost seemed as if his father was showing no mercy, though he knew that wasn't really the case. "If the sickle didn't plug all the time," he complained, "it wouldn't be quite so choppy."

"Let's have a look," dad said. They walked to the machine, and dad's sharp eyes scrutinized every guard and blade. Jed was glad he'd cleaned it when he came home.

"Here's your trouble," dad said. "Two bent guards. Must have hit a rock."

Jed hadn't seen or heard any rocks, but if dad said he'd hit a rock, he probably had. Dad took a pipe and, with some well-placed pressure, soon had the guards bent back in proper shape.

"Watch for rocks," he warned. "They're hard on equipment. And go slow, or you'll send one sailing."

"I will," Jed promised. "If I'd known it was a bent guard, I wouldn't have such a mess out there."

Today the job was much easier. Jed watched carefully for rocks, and soon relaxed. His shoulders didn't ache the way they had earlier, and he could move without his eyes glued to the machine. He gave the tractor a little more fuel, and before long he was buzzing around the field, enjoying the odor of the freshly cut crop as it dropped to the ground behind him.

First-crop hay always went quickly. It was chopped and put in the silo to be fed as haylage. The second crop was more work. It had to be dried, raked, and baled. The piling and unloading were hard work, too, but even then, Jed liked haying. It gave him a good feeling to store crops for the winter.

Jed smiled to himself. Yesterday had been such a trial, and today was so different. What a relief! He glanced to the side, and a flash in midair caught the corner of his eye. Another rock! He ducked instinctively, slammed in the clutch, and waited for the rock to hit the cab window.

7

DREAMING

IT WASN'T A ROCK. It was the female mallard! Her nest was in the field, and, grazed by the mower, she had flown in terror. Scattered feathers dropped to the ground.

Jed shut the machine off and jumped from the cab. A few feet back he found the nest. The eggs had barely been missed.

Jed took his handkerchief and marked the spot. If he cut around it, maybe she would return and hatch the eggs.

"Won't the little ducks die?" Gretchen asked when he told about it at lunch.

"I don't think so," dad said. "If you stay away

from the nest, she'll probably come back and hatch the eggs."

"I'll stay away," Gretchen said. "I promise."

The next weeks flew by rapidly. The garden grew in the hot June sun. Lush strawberries graced the Craig table and satisfied the appetites of those around it. For Jed there was no better treat than the big, red berries piled high on mother's shortcake and topped with mounds of thick whipped cream. When the strawberries quit bearing, the raspberries began. They made his favorite jam. But mother and the girls took care of those. Jed looked forward to the blueberry season when he could help with the picking.

The work load had settled to normal for that time of year. The corn crop, far ahead of normal, was cultivated twice, and the harvesting of the rest of the first hay crop went quickly. By the third week in June they were finished.

Shortly after, most of the family went looking for blueberries. Granddad and Sari stayed at home. Dad drove north to the sandy soil, crossed the Namekagon River, and followed the side roads to blueberry country. There he chose fire lanes to follow until they reached a spot where the blueberry brush appeared.

The day was a breezy one of clouds mixed with sunshine, and as he picked, Jed enjoyed the rustling of the tall Norways and poplar trees far above. Near the ground, however, his hair was barely stirred by the breeze. When the sun broke through on his arms and shoulders, he pulled off his shirt to let it brown his back. When it went under, he welcomed the cooling breeze again.

As he picked, his mind wandered to other places he hoped to visit someday. Jed felt he could learn to live anywhere. Even the sea attracted him.

Presently he heard someone coming.

"Have I got enough for a pie yet?" It was Jared.

"If I've told you once," Jed said, "I've told you a hundred times. It takes four cups."

"Have I got that much?" Jared tipped the pail for him to see.

"No, it's more like three cups," he said, "but you can't stop when you have enough for a pie."

"I know. I think it's better over there." And Jared plunged off to another spot.

In a few moments the first rumblings of thunder sounded overhead. More rain was coming in from the northwest. Jed picked faster, and as a few drops began falling, he worked back toward the truck. By the time he reached the fire lane, the sun was shining again, and he crossed to the opposite side where the berries were bigger. But the sunshine was short-lived; rain clouds continued to gather, and the thunder sounded closer. His father had joined him on that side, and they picked fast to finish before the rain began.

"Run!" dad called suddenly. "Here it comes!"

In the few seconds it took to reach the truck, they were wet. Mother, Gretchen, and Jared came running from the opposite side. Squeezed in the truck cab, they shook the water from their arms and hair.

Dad grinned. "Tough folks we are," he said. "A little moisture, and we're flushed from the bushes like hunted birds."

Everyone laughed.

The rain didn't last long, but it was too wet to continue picking. It was nearly time to leave for home, anyway. Dad started the truck, and as they left the woods, Jed's sharp eyes caught sight of a regal whitetail standing motionless about fifty yards from the trail. "Look," he whispered, "a deer."

His father stopped the truck.

"Is it a buck?" Jared asked.

Jed leaned forward. "I don't see horns, but they'd blend in with the branches, anyway."

"More than likely a doe," dad said. "The bucks are in the velvet now and should be easier to see."

They watched several minutes. Then dad gave a soft, low whistle, and the animal bounded from sight.

"Do you think a bobcat would attack a deer?" Jed asked.

Dad released the clutch, and they were moving again. "Yes, I think so, a small one at least."

Jed swallowed. He didn't care for the sound of that, but he didn't dwell on it. He watched as they wound through the fire lanes, but he did not recognize any of them. At last they came to an unfamiliar stretch of road, and dad turned right.

"Where are we now?" Jared asked.

"I don't know exactly," dad said.

"But according to the sun and the time of day," Jed answered, "we're going south. We should be coming to the Namekagon." He pointed to a sign as it came into view. "See? One-lane bridge ahead."

Jared grinned. "Just like I told you."

"Like *I* told *you*," Jed said.

But dad was serious. "Do you understand why we know we're going south?" he asked.

"Sure," Jared said. "It's afternoon. The sun's in the west and at my right, so we have to be going south."

"Right," dad said. He grinned and winked.

They crossed the Namekagon, and a shady pine campground rested along the shore.

"Ooh," Gretchen sighed. "Look at those lucky ducks. They're tenting."

"Camping," Jared said. "Not *tenting*."

Gretchen swung around. "Why can't we ever go camping?"

Dad scratched his forehead and brushed his hair to one side. "Just out of curiosity, if we *could* take a vacation," he asked, "where would you want to go?"

57

"Disneyland!" Gretchen screeched.

Jared bounced in the seat. "Me, too!"

"Not me," said Jed. "Someplace like Yosemite or Yellowstone."

"Not anywhere in summertime," mother said. "Winter would be much better."

Jed agreed, "But I sure would like to see some of the country."

"Who votes for Disneyland?" Jared asked, and he raised his hand.

Dad grinned again. "Sounds like *everybody* wants a vacation."

8

THE
ANNIVERSARY

NEXT MORNING JED WAS AWAKENED by hushed voices on the bed next to his. He raised his head and managed to open one eye. The girls and Jared were whispering excitedly.

"What's going on?" he asked.

Sari placed her finger on her lips. "Come over here."

Pushing the covers back, Jed staggered across the room and sank onto the edge of the bed.

"How much money do you have?" Jared whispered.

He groaned and rolled over. "Who wants to know?" It was very little, but he didn't intend to lend it to anyone, especially Jared.

"*We* want to know," Sari said. "Thursday is mom and dad's wedding anniversary, and we're going to buy them a wiener roast."

Gretchen stretched herself to all the height she could muster. "It was my idea," she said proudly. "It'll be just like when people are tenting."

"Camping," Jared said.

"I've got $2.15," Sari announced. "Gretchen has 82¢, and Jared has $1.66."

"You've got more than that," Jed said to his brother. He had watched him count his money last week.

Jared picked at the yarn ties of the patchwork quilt. "I spent 89¢ for that licorice when we were in town."

He might have known—Jared and his candy.

"Well, how much have you got?" Gretchen asked.

"I'll have to look." Jed rose and started toward his dresser.

He rummaged through his drawer and found everything he had. "Total of $3.45," he announced. "That do you any good?"

"I think we can manage," Sari said. "That is, if you agree."

"Of course I agree."

"Good. Now all we have to do is get to town. How can we manage that without mom and dad knowing?"

"Can't," Jed said. "Dad would have to know so we could do chores early. Are you sure we have enough money?"

"I think so," Sari said. "We'll add up while we shop and not go over."

After breakfast, while mother and dad were having coffee, the four children approached them together. Gretchen had been elected spokesman, since it was her idea. "For your anniversary present," she announced, "we are going to buy you a wiener roast."

"A wiener roast!" mother exclaimed. "My favorite."

"But we had to tell you, because we have to get the things from town, and you have to do chores early on Thursday so we can sit around and enjoy it."

"And not have to rush back to work," Jed added.

Dad and mother were both smiling. "That sounds like a generous and wonderful invitation," mother said.

"It'll be at the back lake," Sari said, "behind the barn. Dad will have to bring granddad in the truck."

On Wednesday, mother drove to town and waited outside while the children went into the store. At the meat counter, Jed asked for fourteen wieners. "Get a dozen buns," he told the others. "I'll take a slice of bread from home."

"So will I," Sari said. She and Jared found potato

61

chips and corn chips, while Jed and Gretchen chose marshmallows and looked over the selection of soft drinks.

"Oh, there's strawberry!" Gretchen squealed. "I want that!"

Sari and Jared had joined them. "It's not real good," Sari said. "Orange is better."

"But I want strawberry. Strawberries are so good."

"Let her have it," Jed said. "It's her money, too."

They chose seven cans and stood around the grocery cart while Sari added. "We have plenty. It only comes to $5.88."

"You're sure?" Jed asked.

"Of course I'm sure."

The next evening, chores were finished early while Sari and Gretchen packed the supplies in the picnic basket. Then they all headed for the back lake, dad and granddad in the truck, and the others walking. On the way, the children collected small, dead branches to start the fire. They stopped where the sand in the bank was like brown sugar, and a ring of rocks marked the spot for the fire.

Dad arrived with granddad and made him comfortable in his folding chair.

Jed snapped the twigs, arranged them over crumpled paper, and lit them. But as soon as the paper was burned, the fire threatened to die. Most of the wood was wet. A dead oak branch with dry

Jed wished they could sleep by the campfire.

leaves lay nearby. "Get some of those," he called. "Quickly, before it goes out completely."

"Let me help you," dad offered.

"You and mother sit down," Jed said. "This is our treat." He stuffed the dry leaves under the moist wood. They were soon ablaze, and the wood kindled.

Sari unwrapped the hot dogs and arranged them on roasting tongs. The boys roasted them while she and Gretchen did the serving. "We forgot plates," Sari apologized as she handed her mother a hot dog in a napkin.

"This is finger food anyway," mother said. "After an occasion like this, who'd want to do dishes?"

As she began eating, Gretchen looked totally satisfied. "Only the mustard and catsup didn't cost anything," she announced.

"How's that?" dad asked.

"We took them from the refrigerator!"

Everyone laughed.

Jed was proud. He felt the money couldn't have been better spent. He opened the soda, and Gretchen took her first swallow of the strawberry flavor. She wrinkled her face in disappointment. "I'm never going to buy this again," she said. "It isn't very good."

They all relaxed and enjoyed the picnic. Dad leaned against a tree, his hands behind his head. "Funny how everyone gets quiet when they're full."

Mother smiled. "It's being satisfied."

The others were too comfortable to say anything. When only coals were left, Jed opened the marshmallows and threaded them onto sharpened twigs. He toasted them golden brown and passed them around until everyone had enough.

The breeze stilled, the sun sank below the hill, and darkness settled in. Jed was beginning to feel drowsy himself, and he wished they could sleep by the campfire so the spell would not be broken. Momentarily his head nodded, but then, without warning, a piercing scream shattered the night.

Jed's heart leaped to his throat. Terrorized, he froze in place, and Sari stiffened like a board beside him. He had never imagined such fright. For an instant, everything stood still.

In the next second, Gretchen screamed and ripped through the embers as she raced to her father.

SAFE!

MOTHER AND SARI both screamed as dad caught Gretchen in his arms.

"She's burned!" mother yelled.

Jed knew she wasn't, but he couldn't find his voice to say so. His very breath seemed yanked from his insides. The jolt was worse than he'd ever imagined.

Suddenly Jared started to run for home.

"Get back here!" dad yelled.

Gretchen was crying and Sari trembling.

"Calm down," granddad directed. "We'll get in the truck and go home."

Dad started for the truck. "Put the things in the back," he ordered. "Mother, get in the cab." He put Gretchen inside. "Help me with granddad, Jared. Jed, you tend the fire."

Somehow Jed found the strength to move. Everyone did as he was told.

"You drive," dad said to mother. "Sari can squeeze in, too. The boys and I will sit in back."

Jed jumped in and scooted up near the cab. As the truck jerked forward, he grabbed hold of the side. His only thought was to get inside the house.

Mother drove right to the door. Dad carried Gretchen, and Jared followed, leaving Jed to tend to granddad. Sari shook visibly as she walked beside Jed. He was still trembling too as he helped granddad to bed.

He and Jared then found it convenient to go upstairs together. In their room, when Jared wasn't watching, Jed glanced quickly in the mirror. He even looked different, kind of weak and white. He couldn't believe the power the scream had on him.

They climbed into bed, but neither made a move to turn off the light.

"Were you scared?" Jared asked finally.

Jed swallowed. He hated to admit his fear, but he had to tell his brother the truth. Jared could probably tell anyway. "Yeah," he confessed. "I can still feel that cold streak shooting up my spine." It made him shiver all over to remember. Just so

Emery didn't find out. That might be worse than the bobcat itself.

"Boy, am I glad," his brother said. "I thought maybe it was only me and the girls."

Jed shook his head. "I know now why you were so scared this spring."

"I bet Gretchen's glad we're not tenting tonight," Jared added.

Jed closed his eyes and thanked the Lord that they'd gotten back home all right. Then he turned off the light and wiggled deep under the covers. In spite of the scare, he decided, he was glad he'd heard the caterwaul at last. Maybe the threat was as bad as anything. At least now he knew what to expect, and he told himself that the next time wouldn't be so bad.

When Jed looked out the window the next morning, the farm was as calm and peaceful as always. The only motion to catch his eye was the mallard waddling toward the lake—with a row of fuzzy ducklings behind her. Jed ran to scoop Gretchen from her bed. "Come on," he said. "I have something to show you."

Gretchen was so sleepy she could hardly hold onto his neck. "Where are you taking me?"

At the front window, Jed pointed toward the lake. "Look!"

The moment she saw the ducklings, Gretchen was wide-awake. "Ooh, mama, come and see!" she called. "How many are there, Jed?"

He was already counting. "Eight. Every egg hatched. I didn't break one. Now you can watch them all summer."

"That'll be fun," she said. "I'm glad at least *some* eggs take care of themselves."

"What's wrong with eggs?" Jed asked.

Gretchen flopped in a chair. "Nothing, and the hens are fine too, especially the big fat one I call Henrietta. We're friends. But that old rooster is getting bigger and meaner every day. He doesn't like me at all. The day before yesterday he strutted all around the hen house and acted like I had to have his permission to gather the eggs. Yesterday he stood right in the doorway and gave me a mean look." Her small chest sank. "I don't know what he'll do today."

Jed grinned and pulled her hair. "Don't let him bluff you, Shorty. It's your job to get the eggs."

Later that morning, Jed went to sharpen the mower sickle. He pulled the bench and grinding wheel outside the shed for more room and turned on the motor. Sitting on the bench, he held the blade to the wheel. The scrape of metal against stone screeched above the whirring of the revolving wheel. Sparks flew.

He kept the blade to the wheel and was almost finished when he heard a yell above the racket. Jed pulled the sickle away and listened. The screeching ended, but he heard Gretchen scream from behind the barn.

BOBCAT!

Jed's imagination flared. Could it be the bobcat? He threw down the sickle, jumped from the bench, and ran for the barn. Rounding the corner, he stopped in his tracks.

Partway up the corncrib, his sister clung to the side, yelling. Behind her, the old rooster fluttered in the air and pecked at the seat of her jeans. "Stop him!" she screamed. "He's killing me!"

Jed burst out laughing.

"It's not funny!" Gretchen yelled. "It's not funny at all."

Jed ran toward her, and the rooster retreated. Finally Jed managed to stop laughing. "I know it's not funny," he gasped, "but I was imagining the bobcat. And when I saw the rooster, it was such a relief that I couldn't help it."

Gretchen jumped down and stopped crying. She wiped her cheeks and eyes with her shirt. "That rooster went right after me."

"Take the heavy basket tomorrow," Jed said. "Walk right up to him, and if he doesn't move, swing."

Gretchen's big eyes looked very uncertain. "You think I could?"

"Sure. Show him who's boss."

"I would," she said as the last tear trickled from her eye, "if I was sure who was."

The next day Jed hid behind the oak as his little sister headed for the hen house. She planted one stocky leg ahead of the other in a determined rhythm and clutched a heavy basket in both hands. But Jed noticed she wore a hooded sweatshirt tied securely at the chin. At the door she hesitated, then turned the latch and went inside.

Jed ran to the door and pressed his ear against it. He couldn't see, but he could hear. At first there were only Gretchen's steps, slow, then faster. Then he heard flapping wings, hurrying feet, a *whang,* another one, and a wild squawk.

He ran back to the tree and waited. When Gretchen came out, her hood was down, the basket was half-filled with eggs, and Henrietta was perched on her shoulder. At the fence gate, she shoved Henrietta off. "Far as you go, missus. You have scratchin' to do."

JULY 4

WITH THE GENEROUS RAINS, the second crop of hay grew rapidly, and when his father cut part of the first field, the one with the hill he wouldn't plow, Jed went to rake. There he discovered a fox family. The two inquisitive young members darted from their den to watch him each time he circled, and they ducked to safety as he came closer. They entertained him all afternoon.

When Jed told his family about them at suppertime, his father had misgivings. "Holes in the field are hard on equipment, and fox are hard on the partridge and ducks, too. I don't like them around."

"They haven't hurt us, dad," Jed said, "and they're fun to watch."

"That remains to be seen," dad replied. He delayed cutting more hay because the rain continued, and on the Fourth of July the family packed a picnic lunch and drove north. They planned to enjoy the lunch and ride as a holiday celebration, and pick berries if they found some. Granddad's folding wheelchair went into the back, and they all piled into the station wagon.

Everyone enjoyed the early part of the day, but by the time they reached berry country, the air had become hot and humid. It was uncomfortable riding, and finally dad decided to stop and check the surrounding area on foot. Granddad's chair was opened beside the car, and Jed and his father helped him in. When Jed tried to push him under a tree for shade, the wheels dug into the sand, and his dad had to help him.

They found a few scattered berries close by, so mother, Jed, and the other children picked there while dad walked further to see if the crop might improve. But Jed could not keep his mind on picking berries or anything else enjoyable. The weather was too uncomfortable. There was no hint of a breeze to sweep away the hot, muggy air. Deerflies buzzed and circled, then closed in to bite. Jed was glad when it began to rain. It was an excuse to quit and get inside.

Dad returned, and they sat in the car for a while,

but the slow, steady rain increased. When it appeared that it would continue raining all day, dad decided they would drive to Cable. "I've heard there's a good berry crop there," he said. "Maybe we can drive out of the rain and find a dry place to have our lunch."

But it began raining harder. "Appears you'll be breaking the speed limit if you plan to overrun the rain," granddad observed.

Jed laughed. The rain had cooled the air, and even though it was pouring outside, he was enjoying the ride. "Think what we'd have given for a rain like this last year," he said.

"You're right," dad said. "There'll be no complaining."

By the time they reached Hayward, the downpour was so heavy Mr. Craig could hardly see to drive. "There's no use going to Cable," he said. "This rain is covering a wide area. We'll stop at the park, eat lunch in the car or shelter, and then decide what to do."

But before they could reach the park, traffic had slowed to a near standstill. Oncoming cars had their headlights on, but the windshield wipers could not clear the heavy rain fast enough.

Mother was worried. "This is getting worse, John," she said. "We'd better pull off the road."

Dad agreed and inched the car into a parking lot.

"Is anyone hungry?" mother asked. "The lunch is here in the car."

No one wanted to eat. Everyone was more concerned about the darkening sky in the south. Jed glanced at his watch. It was two o'clock in the afternoon, but it looked as if it were nearly night. All traffic had ceased. The wind picked up, and the rain beat unmercifully. When the car began to rock, Gretchen climbed into the front and onto her mother's lap.

Crouched in the seat, Sari folded her hands in her lap and shut her eyes. Jed knew she was praying.

It was more than an hour later when the traffic finally began to move again.

"By the looks of that sky," dad said, "I'm afraid someone to the south was hard hit."

Only a few miles down the road, they witnessed the first results of the storm. Branches and leaves were everywhere. Occasionally trees had snapped, and some were uprooted. Further along, trees lay across the road. Dad had to drive in the ditch to pass the blockage. Where a beautiful wayside had once been, three huge pines were completely destroyed, and beyond that, at a farm pine grove, trees lay over the house, road, and power lines. Even from a distance, the light spots in the dark grove showed distinctly where the timber had been broken.

Along the east side of Sand Lake, damage became more intense. Finally they were stopped by a wall of pine and poplar covering the road. Several people were gathered around.

"You'll have to turn back," one man said to dad. "The road is blocked solid for a half mile ahead." He pointed to a drive nearby. "You can turn there, but don't back too far. The wires are down, and they're live."

"Thanks," Mr. Craig said. He turned the car around, and they drove the several miles back to the north end of the lake and started down the west side. No one talked much as they rode. Jed was certain the big maple on their front lawn would be down. It was a mature tree and had a bad spot on the trunk. But no one wanted to see it go. It had been shading the house since long before he could remember.

As they neared home, however, the damage lessened. Jed craned his neck as they turned the last curve and was the first to see that the old maple still stood. "Yea!" he hollered. "We were spared again!" Only one branch was damaged.

The boys hurried to bring the cows to the barn. But as they approached the barnyard, several trees were down, and the path was blocked. Confused by the change, and thirsty from the heat, the cows swung wide and took off to the back lake to drink.

"Give us a hand," Jed called to the girls, "before they get too spread out." He hurried through the woods partway up the hill, circled to the far side of the cows, and turned them. The usually docile animals were nervous and excited. "Bring them along," Jed called to the others.

Sari, Gretchen, and Jared spread out to keep the cows grouped as they ran, and Jed stayed partway up the hill. "They have to swing south at the fallen trees," he called. "Try to slow them if you can. Don't let them turn."

Things were under control, or so he thought, when a swish rushed through the woods above. Jed's heart skipped a beat. A shriek rang through the hills, and all bedlam broke loose. Both girls screamed and ran, and the cows ran with them.

It was the thing Jed had feared the most. He didn't look back. "Run for your lives!" he yelled as he plunged headlong after the others.

REVENGE

CRASHING DOWN THE HILLSIDE, Jed's arms and legs flew recklessly. Suddenly a branch caught his ankle, and he splattered to the ground.

From somewhere, convulsive laughter broke loose. Jed whirled into a sitting position and saw Emery standing on the ridge. He was doubled over with laughter.

Jed felt as if he'd been kicked by a horse. His stomach knotted and his throat choked. Emery! What was he doing here?

Now Emery churned his arms and bulged his eyes with fright. "Run for your lives!" he jeered, and hee-hawing, he started to slide down the hill.

Jed couldn't stand it. Emery's scream had made a complete fool of him. Jed began to shake, and with every beat of his heart, the blood churned stronger in his veins. With teeth set and fists clenched, he pounded up the hill to pulverize Emery.

He swung once and missed, and Emery's startled face blurred through a greenish haze. Quivering, he swung again just as Jared grabbed him from behind.

Emery grabbed his other arm. "Take it easy, will you? Your mother told me you were here when I came to see the damage, and I thought I'd give you a little thrill. That's all."

Jed struggled fiercely to free himself, and the look on Emery's face turned serious. "H-e-y," he said, "you really think there *is* a bobcat, don't you?"

"Clear out!" Jed heard himself yell. "Just clear out!"

Emery cleared out.

Jed wanted to run and never come back. He'd been made to look ridiculous in front of his brother and sisters, too. He'd lost all respect. He almost wished the bobcat was there to finish him off. But it wasn't.

"Come on," Jared said, "we have to tend to the cows."

Jed almost lashed out at him. Although he managed to steady himself, he was still sick and seething when he reached the barn. The storm had knocked out their electricity, so milking had to be done by hand. He thought of all kinds of degrading things he could do to Emery, but the hard work of hand milking kept him from doing any. Besides, no matter what he might do, it wouldn't make him look any better.

Jed was still upset the next morning, and he couldn't blot revenge from his mind. When he went downstairs, mother and dad were at the kitchen table. Without looking at anyone, Jed pulled out a chair and sat down.

After a while his father spoke. "That was a mean trick Emery played last night," he said.

Jed fingered the silverware before he looked up. "He has lots of mean tricks. When we were out in the woods last spring, he pretended he was going to set them on fire."

"Set the woods on fire!" His mother looked aghast.

Jed felt a stab of regret. Because he was angry, he'd said a little too much. "I guess he really didn't mean it," he added.

"He had matches?" dad asked.

That called for another explanation. "He was smoking."

"Smoking!" His mother looked even more shocked.

Jed turned toward dad. "I wasn't," he said. He wished he hadn't said anything.

Dad stood up and pushed his chair in. "I'm glad. You stay steady." He started toward the door. "Let's go. There's hay to put in."

Jed followed. He was thankful dad hadn't made an issue of the smoking incident, but by the look on his mother's face, he didn't think he had heard the last of it.

Outside, he walked to the flatbed and hoisted himself on near the rack. He couldn't believe how one thing could lead to another until a guy had his neck in a noose and it was ready to tighten. He sighed and waited.

"Jed, hook up the wagon." Dad was waiting on the tractor, and he looked a little irritated.

Jed hadn't even realized the wagon wasn't hooked to the tractor. He jumped down.

"If it's last night you're thinking about," dad said, "forgive and forget. Keep your mind on your work."

Jed nodded, and he meant to try, but it was harder than it sounded. He put the pin in the wagon tongue and climbed aboard. At the field his job was to operate the baler. Because they were working on a sidehill, dad piled the bales. Jed watched the baler eat the hay by steady, chopping mouthfuls and spit it out in neat, rectangular packages. The row of bales on the wagon was stacked neat and straight.

BOBCAT!

Last night's misery stabbed him again. He bet Emery couldn't pile a wagonload of bales if he had to. In fact, he bet he could bale fast enough to bury Emery on the wagon. Jed thought of the startled look on his mother's face when he'd mentioned the smoking, almost as if *he* might be the culprit.

The load on the wagon grew higher, but Jed's imagination was still in command when he turned and suddenly saw a hole behind the tractor. He swerved to avoid it, but the wagon wheel caught it on the low side. He hit the brake and the wagon dipped, the corner hitting the ground.

Jed glanced upward just as the load of bales split down the middle. His dad was thrown from the load, his cap left in midair. Jed saw him land feet first, but the tumbling bales knocked him forward.

Jumping from the tractor, Jed dashed toward his father. Bales had pinned his legs. Jed grabbed and tossed them like empty boxes. "Oh, dad!" he cried. "It was *my* fault. I was thinking about Emery."

Jed wanted to bury his face forever. He was so ashamed. But nothing could change the damage he'd caused. All he could do was to help clean up. At least his father did not seem hurt.

The wagon, however, was badly damaged. While dad rested, Jed went home for another. He saw the two young foxes that were responsible for the hole, but he could hardly blame them. The hole on the hillside was clearly visible. If his mind had been on his job instead of on revenge, he would have swung out in time.

At home he hooked the tractor to another wagon and returned to the field. Many bales were broken and had to be rebaled. Jed piled them on the wagon. It was hot, hard work.

"Are you hurt?" he asked when he saw his father limping.

"Twisted my knee a little is all," dad said.

They cleared the field with one wagon, unloaded at home, and returned for the damaged one. The frame was sprung. Working late, they heated the metal, straightened it, and repaired the wheel and flatbed.

12

THE OLD
SHEEPHERDER

THE NEXT MORNING mother called Jed to the kitchen. Dad was there too, but he didn't say anything. Mother said she was concerned about Jed's temptation to smoke. "Do you understand the health risks?" she asked.

"Yes," Jed said. "We learned about that in school."

"Good health is an outright gift from the Lord," she reminded him. "It's to be appreciated and respected."

"It's one of the responsibilities to yourself and your family," dad added.

Jed understood, and wished he hadn't even mentioned the day in the woods. He had no intention of smoking.

Mother still did not seem satisfied.

"I don't know yet what it is," she said at last, "but there has to be some positive way of showing young people the concrete benefits of not smoking."

The following days, newscasters gave reports of extensive storm damage in the Flambeau River State Forest. When the roads had been cleared, granddad mentioned that he would like to view it firsthand. He had grown up along the Flambeau.

"I think we could go today," dad said. "It's not going to be a good haying day anyway."

With the whole family in the station wagon, dad drove north and east to the forest. Whole sections of land had been stripped. For miles, mutilated trees lay haphazardly on one another. Their root systems were ripped from the ground and left bared to the wind and rain.

Along the river's edge, shoreline sections had been rolled back in furrows as the trees were flattened by the storm's force. Huge fallen pines still emitted their fresh pine scent, but the humbled green branches mingled with the rust-colored bed of dead needles below. Dad stopped the car so they could get out for a better look at the damage.

Jed stood on a bridge and tried to understand. He saw his grandfather raise his face to the wind.

"A sobering sight," he said aloud. "In all my years, I've never seen destruction like this."

"It's hard to understand," dad added. "But it reminds us that no strength on earth endures. The only real strength is God's."

Dad always said that people did more learning in bad times than good, but Jed hoped he could remember God's truths without such another horrible reminder. As he pictured their own forest at home—green, tall, and inviting on the hills above the lake—he wondered what they would do if it were lying flat. He didn't think he could stand to wake in the morning and find it ruined.

Back in the car, they took a different route home. Soon they came to an unfamiliar, desolate-looking ranch where the fields had gone untended for years. The grass in the pastures looked little better than hair on a shedding dog; there was very little new growth, and the sparse, brittle spears of the old grass were valueless.

"An old sheep ranch," dad observed.

Except for a shabby cabin near the road, the buildings were vacant. All were paintless, and a single, broken pine stood guard at the unrepaired gate. Near it, an old man with drooping shoulders leaned heavily on a walking stick. The sagging, rippled brim of his battered hat half-covered his brown, wrinkled face, which reminded Jed of rough, tanned leather. The man stared at their car as dad brought it to a stop.

"Hello," dad said. "I'm John Craig, neighbor about five miles southwest."

Granddad extended his hand through the open back window. "Another Craig; Sam. And your name is—?"

"Hawkins," the old man said. "Ben Hawkins, though I don't know that it makes much difference. Nobody knows me anymore."

"Anything we can do for you?" dad asked.

"No, I've been looking for a missing lamb, but he's been gone several days now; and I hear there's a bobcat around, so it's pretty well settled. You folks seen anything of it?"

At the mention of the bobcat, Jed winced. He'd been praying and trying to work out some solution ever since the wagon episode, and now at least his anger toward Emery had left. That much had been accomplished, but a lot of the problem still remained. If he didn't redeem himself in Emery's eyes before September, he'd be the laughingstock of the whole school. Emery would see to that.

"Haven't seen it," dad said, "but we've heard it. I didn't know there were sheep here anymore."

"Only a couple," Ben said. He shifted the stick to his other hand and used it for a pointer. "I don't do much anymore but keep an eye on the place for my nephew. He doesn't come here often."

"Long as we can't help," dad said, "we'll be going. We have chores to do yet, but we'll stop again when we come this way."

"Wish you would," Ben said.

"And if you come our way, look us up."

Ben looked doubtful. "They still let me drive the old truck a few miles, but I ain't had her out of the shed in quite a spell. Nowhere to go, but I'll see."

Mrs. Craig leaned across the seat toward him. "Come at mealtime. There's always room for one more."

Old Ben stepped backward, raised his hand in good-bye, and limped slowly from the gate.

As Jed turned to watch, his heart went out to the old man. He had never known anyone so alone. Besides that, how could an old man protect himself or his sheep from a bobcat? As much as Jed disliked the idea, he wished the cat would come back near them. Going after it would be the only way to prove himself.

The next time *will* be different, he promised.

13

ALONE
WITH THE
BOBCAT

JED WAS BARELY ROUSING next morning when he heard the screen door shut softly. After waiting and hearing nothing further, he tiptoed downstairs to look out the window. Near the morning glories, granddad reached out slowly and fingered the first blossoms of the morning.

Hearing someone on the stairs, Jed turned to see Sari behind him. She touched his arm. "I saw granddad from the upstairs window. Should we go out so he won't be alone?"

Jed felt sure that the river and the forest had revived granddad's memories of his childhood and his life as a young man. "No," he said softly. "I don't think he feels alone just now."

In early August, Jed took his gun rack to exhibit at the county fair, and Sari took a jumper she had made. Though he hoped for a blue ribbon, Jed wasn't confident. He'd not had time enough to spend on the sanding and varnishing, and secretly he hoped more for a blue ribbon for Sari than for himself.

When they arrived at the fair after the judging, they went right to the clothing exhibit. Jed was the first to see the red ribbon on Sari's jumper, and he hoped she wouldn't be too disappointed.

When Sari saw it, she clapped her hands. "Oh, good. I prayed it wouldn't be pink. I hate to always be the worst."

"Worst?" Jed said. "Pink doesn't mean worst. It simply means others are more exact."

"That's an accurate explanation," mother said.

Jed felt quite grown-up. He ran to the wood-working display with Jared behind him. Since Sari's ribbon was red, he didn't want his to be blue. It wasn't. It was pink, and he felt a pang of what Sari had described.

Jared didn't say anything.

The others joined them, and when Gretchen saw the ribbon, tears swelled in her eyes. "It's not the worst, is it, Jed?"

He swallowed hard.

She turned to grandfather. "You'll still let him put your gun on it, won't you?"

Granddad looked very serious. "No," he said, "I don't believe I will."

Jed didn't know what to say. His mouth dropped open. He'd never expected—

"I'll let him put *his* gun on it," granddad said. "The Winchester belongs to you, Jed."

"Granddad!" He'd wanted the rifle since last fall. But he was a little afraid that his grandfather was feeling sorry for him, and he didn't want that. He couldn't explain his jumbled feelings, so he simply acknowledged the gift. "It's better than a hundred blue ribbons," he said, and he meant it.

After some rides, they ate popcorn, drank orange soda, and Gretchen had cotton candy. Later they watched the fireworks that concluded the grandstand entertainment, and then it was time to start home. Jed sat in front with his parents because Gretchen said she wanted to sleep on granddad's lap.

Sari and Jared were soon asleep too, but Jed stayed awake all the way. They were nearly home, driving beside the lake, when he saw two bright eyes shining on the roadside. "A fox," dad said, and it darted across the road in front of them. "A good-sized one, too. Wonder what he's been up to?"

Mother looked after him suspiciously. "I hope the hen house door is closed."

"I'm sure it is," Jed said. "Gretchen takes good care of those chickens."

"She does, but she was so excited about the fair

she could have forgotten. Would you check for sure while I get these sleeping children to bed?"

"All right. I will."

When dad stopped the car and carried Gretchen into the house, Jed took his grandfather's wheelchair from the back and helped him inside. Now that he was home, Jed was tired, too. By the time he finished helping granddad, Jared had stumbled into the house but was too groggy to manage the stairs by himself. Jed helped him climb up and opened the door to their room. Inside, Jared flopped on the bed and pulled up his legs.

"Pull open your bed and get your pajamas on," Jed said, but his brother didn't answer. Jed walked over to pull him upright, but he was too tired himself. Instead, he took a blanket from the closet and covered Jared.

Crawling into his own pajamas, Jed said a short prayer, dived into bed, and shivered. He was always cold when he was tired. He pulled the covers around his ears and wrinkled the pillow just right. Sometimes during the day, especially since they had talked about it, he wished they were on a trip. It would be nice to get away—anywhere. But when night and weariness came, he was glad for home and his own bed.

He was almost asleep when he remembered the hen house door.

Jed threw the covers back quickly, before he was tempted to forget it, slipped into a jacket, and picked up his shoes. The house was quiet. He wiggled his bare feet into the shoes and headed for the hen house.

The yard light brightened his way, and he watched his shadow until he rounded the corner of the barn. Then it was dark. He passed the big oak, bumped into the fence before he saw it, and followed it to the gate. At least that was shut, but he couldn't see further. He went right up to the hen house door and put his hand on it before he could tell.

It was shut. He could just as well have stayed in bed. His hand was still on the latch when the dreaded shriek of the cat pierced the night. Jed's heart sprang in his chest. It bolted his body rigid and flattened him against the door. His throat went dry and his mind blank.

The shriek knifed again, from the oak! Like a rifle bullet, Jed shot forward. Unable to see, he hit the fence, glanced through the gate, and clipped the corner of the barn. His legs couldn't move fast enough as he ripped for the house. Terror streaked beside him. Flog barked as he shot past her, flew up the steps in one mighty leap, and burst through the door. Trembling and weak, he collapsed against it.

14

A LITTLE CONFIDENCE

JED COULD BARELY KEEP his knees from buckling. But the house was still. No one had heard! Cold and shaking, he clung to the banister and climbed the stairs to his room. He remembered that he hadn't closed the fence gate, but he wasn't going back for anything.

Trembling violently, he climbed into bed and buried his face in the pillow. He had been so *sure* that the next time would be different!

His insides refused to calm down. He rolled this way and that in the bed; but no matter what he tried, he was unable to shake the grating gnaw inside him. He couldn't hide from . . . from what? he asked himself at last. What did he need to hide from? Not from the bobcat; he was safe from him.

Not from what Emery or his parents or the rest of the family would think; none of them knew anything about tonight. He squeezed his eyes shut, and the gnawing accelerated until it scraped out the humiliating truth. He was hiding from his own fear.

He gradually calmed down and got to sleep. He did not awaken in the morning until he felt someone shaking him. When he rolled over, he saw his dad holding out a glass of chocolate milk.

"Good morning. It was hard for me to wake up, too." He grinned and pointed to a cup of steaming coffee on the dresser. "Too much fair."

Jed pulled himself up in the bed and took the milk. "Thanks, dad." He thought immediately of the bobcat. He knew he should tell his father—it was so close—but he was too ashamed to admit that he had fled in blind fright.

"Did you enjoy the fair?" dad asked.

"It was fun, watching Gretchen especially."

Dad smiled. "She enjoys everything."

Right now, Jed wasn't enjoying much of anything. When there was a free moment during chores, he slipped away and checked the hen house. Everything was normal. He closed the door and fence gate and left, deciding definitely not to tell at all. There were some things you had to face alone.

That evening, as soon as he could, he crept off to his room, but not to sleep. Instead, he sat by the window facing the lake and studied his problem. Surely, he thought, there had to be some way to reverse the pendulum that was swinging in the wrong direction for him. Somehow he had to conquer his fear. He wished he could simply charge out after the bobcat, but he knew that wouldn't work. He could spend days and never see the animal, and he didn't have that kind of time. The time had to be when the bobcat was there, and he had to be ready. That seemed to be his major problem; he was never ready.

When his father called next morning, Jed pulled on jeans, shirt, and shoes and went out into the damp, early morning. It was a beautiful time of day—quiet, clear, and fresh. Not a leaf stirred, and standing alone by the lake, he felt quite isolated from everything, even his own troubles. He stopped as he noticed the mallard swim from the shore, followed by the row of growing ducklings, but the row seemed short. He counted.

Only six. Two ducklings were missing.

Jed thought immediately of the fox and knew what had happened. He hated to tell Gretchen.

But he didn't have to. He was finishing in the barn when she ran in.

"Jed," she called. "Two ducklings are gone. They're not anywhere. What could have happened?"

Jed sat down on a bale of straw. Problems were everywhere, but he couldn't protect her from the truth. "I think it was the fox," he said. "We saw him on the road the night we came from the fair. I'm sorry."

His little sister looked horrified. "You mean he *ate* them?"

"It's the way with wild things," Jed explained. "An animal lives by instinct. He looks out only for himself."

"I wouldn't do that."

"You're not a wild thing. God gave you a conscience and a soul. You have to do right by everybody and everything."

Her small shoulders drooped. She thought a moment more and announced her decision. "Then," she said, "we're going to catch the rest of them and protect them. Will you help me?"

Jed didn't really feel like helping anyone; he had enough of his own troubles. But he could hardly explain that to her, so he tried the easy way out. "I don't know how we'd do it. They're wild. I can't catch them."

Gretchen stamped her foot in front of him. "Yes, you can. I didn't think I could face that old rooster either, but when I made up my mind, I did." Her eyes narrowed. "You aren't scared of that fox, are you?"

That stung a little. "No," Jed snapped. "I'm not. Get a box and string and come to the lake."

Gretchen ran for the supplies and soon was back.

Jed didn't say much. Turning the box on its side,

he put feed in it and rigged the string over a tree branch, to be released when the ducks entered. "All we can do is try," he said. At least it would satisfy his sister.

They took turns standing guard, but when night came, the ducks were still on the water.

In the morning there were five left, and Jed felt guilty. He hadn't tried very hard. He pointed to the half-sunken log wedged into the shore where the ducks often gathered. "They sit there a lot. We'll push it out from shore and tie it with a rope. Maybe they'll recognize that as a safe place to roost. I don't think the fox could get them there."

They worked with the log every spare minute Jed had during the day and finally loosened the one end from its embedded spot in the shore. With a short twine, they anchored it to a tree so it would not drift too far away. But the following morning, there were only four ducklings.

Gretchen cried and could not be comforted, and Jed knew he had to be more resourceful. He tried to think of a solution. Ducks weren't too much different than anything else. They had to like feed. "Maybe it was too dark in the box," he said. "We'll make one out of chicken wire."

He pounded together a frame of wood and used fence staples to fasten chicken wire all around. They sprinkled ground feed and corn in a path to the opening. A string was attached to the cover as before, and Gretchen volunteered to stand watch from behind the tree trunk, since Jed had to work.

He and his father spent all day in the oats field. When they came home for supper, he was worn-out, but he ran to the tree. Gretchen was still behind it, and the ducks were still on the lake.

"Didn't they eat it?" he asked, pointing to the feed.

"Just up to the cage. They wouldn't go inside."

"But the feed is still there."

"I kept sprinkling more."

Jed shook his head. "They're not hungry now," he said. "Come to supper."

Reluctantly, Gretchen followed him inside.

After milking, Jed found a thin wire and propped the cage flap gingerly. "We can't watch all night," he said. "If they should hit this going in, it'll drop and catch them."

Gretchen looked discouraged, but she hoped out loud. "Maybe we'll get the fox. That would fix everything."

"Maybe," Jed said, but he knew that trap was never going to catch any fox.

He was still sleeping in the morning when Gretchen ran into his room crying. She threw her-self on his bed and sobbed through her tears. "The mother duck is gone. I'm never going outside again, not as long as I live."

Jed felt nearly as badly as she did. He tried to get her to change her mind, but she wouldn't, so he went outside alone, feeling very defeated. *Catch a fox or a bobcat?* he thought. *I can't even catch a duck.*

Then he had an idea. The ducks were afraid too, and he had to think of some way to dispel their fears. That was it! Henrietta! He ran to the house for more string, to the barn for feed, and to the hen house for Henrietta. It would have been easier for Gretchen since she and the hen were best friends, but Jed managed.

Back near the lake, he sprinkled a *little* feed on the path—so the ducks would still be hungry—and a lot inside. Then he opened the flap, put Henrietta inside, and tied her by one leg with a short string. She didn't mind a bit. She had plenty of room and plenty to eat. Then he hid behind the tree.

Before long, he saw them, four ducklings waddling to the cage, eating their way as they went. He watched and waited. Presently they were inside. He released the string, and the flap snapped shut.

Jed ran for the house. "Gretchen!" he yelled. "I've got them! Come and see."

Everybody heard. They all ran out. Granddad came in his wheelchair. Gretchen threw her arms around his neck and kissed him. "How did you do it?" she cried.

Jed just grinned. "Another few hours, and I'd have had the fox too."

"I believe it," dad said. "With that hen in there, I believe it."

15

THE SOUTH PASTURE

JED FELT BETTER. His small success had restored some self-confidence, and he was not as occupied with his fears of the bobcat. Anyway, he decided, it was the initial jolt that panicked him every time. If he could just keep his head when he heard it again, things would be better. But September and school were coming closer, and time was running out.

A few days later he came home from the field early to begin chores while dad finished the baling. Jared was raking another field of cut hay. They didn't plan to eat supper until after milking, but Jed stopped at the house for a drink of water. Mother was rolling pie crust, but otherwise it was unusually quiet. "Where is everyone?" he asked.

"Granddad's napping, and Sari wanted blackberry pie, so she and Gretchen went to the pasture to pick. I hope they're back soon. I'm ready for the berries."

Jed's hand stopped halfway to his mouth. His heart jumped too. "What pasture?" he asked.

"Right out behind the barn," mother said. "I thought it would be safe. We haven't heard anything of that bobcat in over a month."

Jed knew better, much better. He was the only one who did. But since his sisters were already gone, there was no use alarming anyone else. He tried to sound unconcerned. "I'm off to start chores. See you later."

But as soon as he was out of sight, he ran like a racehorse. Nearing the barn, he heard Gretchen's voice, and he stopped running. What a relief. He was already sweating.

"Henrietta, please come down," she begged. "Be careful, Sari."

Jed rounded the corner of the barn and saw Gretchen standing at the base of the big oak, looking up into the tree. "What's going on?" he asked.

"It's that stubborn Henrietta," Gretchen complained. "She won't come down, and I have to put her away for the night."

Jed looked to where the hen was perched far out on one of the lower limbs. Sari, in jeans and sweatshirt, stood trembling on the same limb near the

"She won't come down," Gretchen complained.

trunk. He was more concerned about Sari than Henrietta. "What do you think you're doing?" he asked. "Come down." Sari was no tree climber.

"I'm rescuing Henrietta," she announced without looking at him. "She's throwing a tantrum because Gretchen's giving the ducks all the attention. And," she added, "I won't come down."

That didn't sound like Sari. "Come down," he said again. "I'll get her."

Sari shook her head. "I won't. Everybody but me gets to do something exciting. Jared drives the tractor, Gretchen tames roosters, you do all kinds of things, and I never get to do anything." She stared deliberately down at him. "I am going to rescue Henrietta."

Jed was surprised. Sari certainly wasn't acting like herself, but it was good to see her with a little grit.

"How are you going to get out there?" he asked.

"Sit down and inch my way out."

"How did she get up there?" Jed asked Gretchen.

"Shinnied her way up, like you and Jared do."

Jed couldn't believe it. If she could do that, getting out to Henrietta shouldn't be much of a problem. "Go ahead," he said.

Sari eased herself forward and, with both hands, pulled her frame along like a regular tree climber.

Jed grinned and winked at his little sister. "Where are the berries?" he asked.

Gretchen pointed to buckets near the fence. "But

not quite enough for the pies. We have to go back tomorrow."

Jed felt another twinge. They couldn't do that. If something happened . . . He was trying to think of what to say when a cracking sound came from the tree. The branch snapped, and Sari plummeted to the ground. In the air, Henrietta squawked and flapped her wings.

Jed ran to his sister. She lay in a crumpled heap. Her face was white, and her eyes partly closed. "Sari," he called, leaning over her. "Sari."

Gretchen stood with hands over her mouth. "Oh, Jed, is she dead?"

"I don't think so," he said. "Run for mother."

Sari didn't stir, and Jed was afraid to move her. He kept calling her name. The minutes dragged until he heard his mother running toward them. "She fell from the tree," he said. "The branch broke, and she came down."

Mother knelt beside him and put her fingers on Sari's wrist. "Get dad," she said, "and a blanket."

Dad was driving in with a load, and Jed raced toward him. "Come quickly," he called. "Sari's hurt behind the barn." He grabbed a blanket from the house and ran behind dad to where his injured sister lay.

"I don't know how badly she's hurt," mother said. "She won't answer me."

"Sari!" dad called loudly.

Her eyelids fluttered.

"She was in the tree," Jed said. "The branch broke and she fell."

Gretchen was crying. "Henrietta was up there," she sobbed. "She was trying to get her for me."

"We'd better have the doctor check for broken bones," dad said. "It could be shock. I'll bring the car."

Jared had come up beside them. Sari opened her eyes, but they looked blank, and she still did not say anything. Dad and mother placed her in the back seat of the car.

"We'll take care of the milking," Jed said to his father.

Dad nodded and mother looked relieved. She sat in the back seat to tend Sari, and dad drove from the yard.

Gretchen was still crying, but Jed didn't have time for her. "Go to the house with granddad," he said. "We have work to do." He felt for the first time the full responsibility of the chores and milking. It would be a big job, but he was sure they could manage. He hurried toward the barn and began giving directions. "You do the feeding," he said to Jared, "and I'll do the milking."

Inside the milk house, he readied the buckets and carried them to the barn. The cows behaved well, and putting the milkers on was easy, but when the buckets were filled, they were heavy, and it seemed as if each succeeding one became heavier.

An hour and a half later, when he finally finished, his arms felt like jelly. Jared trailed behind him as he walked to the house. But in spite of being tired and hungry, Jed felt a sense of pride in being able to take over when necessary. Dad would be proud of him.

Granddad was waiting on the porch. "Where's Gretchen?" he asked as they approached.

Jed stopped short. "I sent her to the house. Isn't she here?"

"She was, but she said she had to have a few more berries so there would be pie for Sari. When she didn't come back, I thought she had stopped at the barn to wait for you."

"When did she go?" Jed asked.

"Almost right away. She insisted it was her fault Sari was hurt, and she had to do something for her."

Jed's throat went dry. He glanced at his watch. It would soon be dark. He whirled to head for the pasture, but turned and ran into the house instead. This time he'd be prepared. He grabbed the rifle and the shells, and the door slammed behind him. "I'm taking Flog," he said, and he ran to unsnap the chain.

"I'll go with you," Jared said.

Jed started to say no, but from the look on Jared's face, he realized his brother felt some of the same responsibility. Besides, two could cover more ground. "Come on," he said. Turning to granddad, he added, "If she should come back, have her sound the truck horn three times in a row."

He hurried toward the south pasture, the place where the blackberries usually grew the best. A stiff breeze blew from the north, and it was cool. The first bushes were stripped of ripe berries. The boys hurried on. Further away, others had been picked too, and Jed spotted tracks across a wet area into the woods. Flog sniffed the ground and ran ahead.

Jed stopped and called, but no one answered. "Look farther south in the pasture," he said to Jared.

He went but was soon back. "The berries are ripe," he said, "but they're still there."

Jed ran up the hill to a small, overgrown field that was no longer in use. He combed it like a bird dog. Berries had been picked. He saw broken twigs and small tracks. "She's been here!" he shouted. "Check the edges for further signs."

They took turns calling as they searched. Near the south edge of the clearing, Jed stopped short. A bucket, partly filled, sat in the long grass. "Look!" he called. "Her bucket. She must have realized she was lost and become frightened, or she wouldn't have forgotten the berries."

Jed shivered. The thought of his little sister lost sent a cold tremor vibrating clear through his bones. The wind had picked up. It was getting colder and darker.

"Which way would she go?" he wondered aloud.

Jared answered without hesitation. "That way." He pointed straight south.

"Why?" Jed asked.

"Because it's easier."

"But if she were thinking—"

"I didn't think when I was lost," Jared said. "I was scared. I just ran."

The vision of the night at the hen house flashed through Jed's mind. Gretchen *wouldn't* be thinking. But he was in charge, and this time it was his job to do just that—*think,* no matter what happened. South was downhill, and the wind was with her. It would be easier. "You're right, Jared," he said. "Come on."

Flog had been all over the field with her nose to the ground, and she started down the hill with them. All Jed could hear were leaves crackling and twigs snapping underfoot. He stopped to listen, and Jared stopped too. "Gretchen!" he yelled.

He ran again, through the dip before the main descent, and his brother followed. He cupped his hands to call, and at that moment the scream of the cat drilled the woods. Jed's heart leaped, and for a second his body stiffened. It was that initial shock again.

Then he heard another scream and knew it was Gretchen. He raced down the hill. "It's Jed!" he yelled. "Where are you?"

A small figure crouched between two logs

jumped up and ran toward him. Jed grabbed his little sister in his arms. "Thank God you're safe," he whispered.

There was another rush, and Flog hit trail. Gretchen clung to him in desperation. Jed looked into his little sister's tear-stained face and pleading eyes. There was no one else to protect her. She was his responsibility.

"That shriek is only a noise," he said. "Noise can't hurt you." Somehow, saying that calmed him as well. It wasn't the noise, only the animal he had to contend with.

He heard Flog ahead, and the rifle stood ready at his side. As he ran his hand over the barrel and gripped the stock more firmly, the rich taste of victory seeped to his tongue. For a moment he relished its flavor.

That bobcat had terrorized him long enough!

Once Jed had made up his mind, there was no time to lose. He put Gretchen down and placed her hand in Jared's. "You know the way home," he said to his brother. "Take her back."

16

THE
BOBCAT
AT LAST

JED TURNED AND RAN up the hill. There was no need to listen. Flog was trailing, and the bobcat was heading south. At the ridge he swung to the logging trail for easier traveling. He might have to go a long way, but he was prepared to stick it out.

Hurrying through the natural dip beyond the twin oaks he and his father had cut last season, he took a skidway to shorten the distance around the next bend. The huge rock bulldozed out at the landing loomed shadowy ahead. He took another shortcut past it and the virgin pine stump that was dad's favorite deer stand, his confidence growing stronger all the time.

BOBCAT!

He was glad he hadn't told anyone about the cat being in the area again. There were some things dads couldn't help with anyway—like how you felt about yourself—and now he had his chance alone. It would settle the thing with Emery too, but somehow that no longer seemed so important.

He hurried through the shallow swamp and topped the knoll where the half-burned pine, remnant of an earlier fire, still stood erect. It was another of his landmarks. At the south survey line he crossed the fill where their logging trail met the Daagers'. His dad had asked for the link several years ago when his own steep road was badly washed, and Mr. Daager had given permission.

Flog sounded fresh and determined, and Jed pictured the cat tiring ahead. He clapped his pocket to feel the reserve of shells and took a two-handed grip on the rifle.

Cresting the next rise, the moon rose yellow above the trees, and the shadows spread before him. It became easier to see.

Right at the clearing above the drop to the Daager farm, the dog swung sharply east, almost doubling back. Confused, Jed stopped. Most animals preferred to be downwind from a pursuer. Maybe bobcats were different, he thought. He turned to make the swing, but something out of the ordinary caught his attention. He glanced again toward the familiar buildings silhouetted against the deep blue sky. There were the house and shed,

This time—the bobcat would be his.

silo and corncrib, the long barn, and—

Then he saw it: a huge, black cloud rolling from the haymow.

Jed stopped short. It couldn't be! He wheeled and denied that he'd seen it. Nothing could stop him now.

But something inside made him stop. How could he pretend there was no danger below? He turned again. It was there, real! Soon the Daagers' barn would be on fire. That was why the bobcat had turned.

The bobcat! he thought. His one chance after months of torture, and he'd finally mustered the courage. If he didn't go on now, he'd lose the trail.

The cat let loose a terrible shriek, and Jed withstood the shock. His mind kept working, and then he knew. He wasn't afraid. There was no need for proof—not for Emery, not for his family, and not for himself. He still wanted to get the bobcat, but was it selfish? Ahead, Flog barked, and he almost followed, but somehow dad's words filtered through the desire and echoed in his ears, "Sometimes you have to put your own ambitions aside. It isn't always easy."

A cow bellowed in the barn, and the smoke rolled heavier. What was the right thing to do? Irritating as he was, Emery was still his friend. The Daagers were their neighbors—good neighbors, dad had said. If the barn went up, it meant their livelihood.

Jed squeezed his eyes shut to aid his thinking. It

wasn't easy after all this time, after all this struggle. But he knew what he had to do.

He dropped the rifle and raced down the hill for the barn—when a dark figure leaped from the haymow. It was Emery. Something small dropped from his hand as he landed. For a moment, Jed's breath caught. He hesitated, but ran on.

"Fire!" he screamed and ran into the barn. The thick smoke made it hard to see, but he began working down the row of stalls, releasing the cows. By the time he got to the end, he was gasping for breath. He pushed and shoved the last of the herd toward the fresh air beyond the door.

Just then Emery and Mr. Daager came running. The flames began shooting through the barn roof into the night sky, and the three of them stood watching. There was nothing more they could do; they heard the upper floor collapse and knew that the barn would burn to the ground.

A car came racing into the driveway, and Jed's dad jumped out. "What happened?"

Emery said nothing. Mr. Daager wiped his forehead with his sleeve and said, "Well, if it hadn't been for Jed, I'd have lost the cattle besides."

"How did you get here, son?" dad wanted to know.

"I was trailing the bobcat when I saw the smoke. My rifle is still up on the hill."

They stayed at the barn for a long time, doing

what they could to make sure the fire didn't spread. Finally, when Jed and his father prepared to leave, Mr. Daager said quietly, "Sure do appreciate you coming to help us." He was somehow a different man.

Jed rose and walked to the car with his father. He was very tired. The bobcat was gone, and so was his chance, but somehow Jed didn't feel cheated. The Lord had guided him to do the right thing, even when he didn't want to. Satisfied, he eased his head against the seat and rested.

Jed came downstairs in the morning just as Harold Daager entered the kitchen. Emery was behind him, but he was quiet.

Mr. Daager handed Jed the rifle, which he'd found in the daylight. "I've been in town already, and there's quite a stir. The newspaper's getting pictures of the bobcat. It was old Ben Hawkins from the sheep ranch that got him." He nodded. "With your dog. He'll be here as soon as folks give him a chance. He's pretty busy."

He shook hands and left, but Jed barely noticed. He could hardly believe what he'd heard. The sad, old man whom nobody knew—and now he was somebody. He couldn't have been more pleased for anyone else in the world.

"There's something more," mother said. Smiling, she took a glass jar from the cupboard and held it high. "A dollar a day goes inside. It's money saved because your father and I choose not to smoke." She paused. "Next year, there'll be a winter vacation."

A winter vacation!

All this and the bobcat besides! His grandfather winked, and Jed grinned widely. "I can't wait for Ben," he said. "I want to get one good look at that bobcat when it can't yell back."